P9-CCG-616

This magical book belongs to

_____

By Grace Maccarone
Illustrated by Bill Langley and Paul Edwards

Mickey's Halloween Mystery

Mystery at the Haunted Hotel
The Case of the Missing Hat

Mystery at the Haunted Hotel

"Hurray!" shouted Morty. "We're on our way!"

"We're on our way to a haunted holiday!" Ferdie sang.

"Hop in the car, Pluto," Mickey said. "Then we'll be off to Haunted Hollow, the spookiest Halloween town of all time."

"Do you think we'll see a real ghost?" Morty asked.

Mickey laughed. "There's no such thing as a real ghost."

After a long drive, Mickey, Pluto, and the boys arrived at
the Haunted Hotel in Haunted Hollow.

"This place sure is creepy," said Morty.

"I'll bet there are secret passageways and everything," said Ferdie.
Mickey shivered as he felt a finger tap him on the shoulder.

"I am Frank N. Stein. I hope to make your stay…most interesting,"
the manager said as he handed Mickey the key to their room.

"Gee, thanks," said Mickey.

"Here is our room," said Morty. "Number thirteen."

"I can't see a thing," Mickey said as he walked in.
"Someone find a light."

"This must be it," said Ferdie as he flipped a switch. But
the light did not go on. Instead they heard a strange noise.
Urrrghsloooopsqueeek!

"I guess this light switch doesn't work," said Ferdie.

Finally, Ferdie found one that did.

"Wow!" said Morty. "This place is spooky! Look at all those cobwebs."

"How do you like it, Pluto?" Mickey asked. "Pluto? Where are you?"

Mickey and the boys searched the room. They looked behind the curtains, under the bed, and in the bathroom. But they could not find him. Pluto was gone!

"Have you seen our dog?" Mickey asked Frank N. Stein.
"He seems to have disappeared."

"Disappeared…" Frank repeated. "Perhaps you should
talk to Mr. Invisible. He knows about disappearing."

"Can you help us find our dog?" Mickey asked Mr. Invisible. "He seems to have disappeared."

"A dog?" said Mr. Invisible. "I have not seen him. But perhaps you should ask the Werewolf. He knows many dogs."

"I have not seen your dog," said the Werewolf. "But I would love to meet him."

"Allow me to introduce myself," said a man in a long cape. "I am Count Vampire. Would your dog happen to be a *blood*hound?"

"No," said Mickey.

"Then I'm afraid I cannot help you," said the Count.

Mickey and the boys searched and searched, but no one had seen Pluto. They returned to their room and sadly went to bed. Morty sighed, Ferdie sniffed, and Mickey shed a tear. Then Mickey turned out the light, but he could not sleep.

Suddenly, they heard a howl.

Owowooooooo! Owowooooooo!

"It *is* a ghost," said Morty.

"Don't be silly. There's no such thing as a ghost," said Mickey. "I think."

Owowooooooo! Owowooooooo!

"It *is* a ghost!" said Morty, and he jumped up to flip on the light switch.

"That switch doesn't work," Ferdie reminded him as he turned on the bedside lamp.

But all of a sudden they heard that strange noise again. *Urrrghslooopsqueeek!*

Then a secret door slowly opened…with Pluto right behind it!

Pluto howled with happiness. "*Owowooooooo!*"

"I guess that light switch that doesn't work isn't a light switch at all," said Mickey. "It must control the secret sliding door."

Mickey and the boys gave Pluto a big hug.
"See, boys," said Mickey. "I told you there was no such thing as a ghost."
"Owowoooooo!" Pluto howled in agreement.

The Case of the Missing Hat

Detective Minnie Mouse looked out her office window. The flowers were in bloom, and the birds were singing as they built their nests.

Suddenly, Donald Duck burst in, making lots of noise.

"Calm down, Donald," said Minnie. "I can't understand a word you are saying."

Donald pointed to his bare head. Finally, Minnie understood.
"Your sailor hat!" she said. "It's missing!"

"Yes, yes, yes, yes!" Donald jumped up and down. "I'm
getting an award tomorrow, and I have to wear my hat to the
party they are having for me. No one will know me without
my sailor hat," Donald said. "I won't even know myself!"

"Leave it to me," said Minnie. "I'll find your sailor hat."
First they went to Mickey's house.
"Look!" said Minnie. "Look behind that shade."
Donald saw a familiar shadow. "My hat!" he said.
"We caught you, Mickey Mouse," Minnie said.

But when they went inside, the shadow was just a bowl of fruit.

Then they went to Goofy's house.

"Look!" said Minnie. "Look behind the curtain."

Once again Donald saw a familiar shadow. "My hat!" he said.

"We caught you, Goofy," Minnie said.

But the shadow was only the sleeping puppy that Goofy was taking care of.

Next they went to Pluto's house.
"Look!" said Minnie. "Look in the doorway."
Once more Donald saw a familiar shadow. "My hat!"
he said.
"We caught you, Pluto," said Minnie.

But the shadow was Pluto's dog dish.

"I give up," said Donald Duck, and he went home.
But detective Minnie Mouse would not quit. First she looked up. Then she looked down. Then she looked up again. There, in the tree, was Donald Duck's sailor hat with three tiny eggs in it. A family of robins was using it as a nest.

Minnie rushed off to find Donald. When they returned, three tiny beaks were poking their way out of the eggs.

"Sorry, Mother Robin," said Minnie Mouse, "but that nest—er, hat you have there belongs to this gentleman."

Mother Robin was very worried. Her babies were too small to be moved.

Three little open beaks pointed in Donald's direction, and a tear rolled down his cheek.

"Never mind, Minnie," Donald said. "They can have my hat for as long as they need it."

"But what will you wear to your party?" Minnie asked.

Donald gathered a bunch of twigs and put them on his head. "If they can use my hat as a nest," said Donald, "I can wear a nest as a hat!"

And they all laughed.